TREASURE ISLAND

WRITTEN BY
CAVAN SCOTT

PUFFIN

PUFFIN BOOKS

Published by the Penguin Group
Penguin Books Ltd, 80 Strand, London WC2R 0RL, England
Penguin Group (USA) Inc., 375 Hudson Street, New York, New York 10014, USA
Penguin Group (Canada), 90 Eglinton Avenue East, Suite 700, Toronto, Ontario, Canada M4P 2Y3
(a division of Pearson Penguin Canada Inc.)
Penguin Ireland, 25 St Stephen's Green, Dublin 2, Ireland (a division of Penguin Books Ltd)
Penguin Group (Australia), 707 Collins Street, Melbourne, Victoria 3008, Australia
(a division of Pearson Australia Group Pty Ltd)
Penguin Books India Pvt Ltd, 11 Community Centre, Panchsheel Park, New Delhi – 110 017, India
Penguin Group (NZ), 67 Apollo Drive, Rosedale, Auckland 0632, New Zealand
(a division of Pearson New Zealand Ltd)
Penguin Books (South Africa) (Pty) Ltd, Block D, Rosebank Office Park, 181 Jan Smuts Avenue, Parktown North, Gauteng
2193, South Africa

Penguin Books Ltd, Registered Offices: 80 Strand, London WC2R 0RL, England

puffinbooks.com

First published 2014
001

Written by Cavan Scott
Illustrations by Rory Walker

© 2009–2014 Rovio Entertainment Ltd.
Rovio, Angry Birds, Bad Piggies, Mighty Eagle and all related titles, logos
and characters are trademarks of Rovio Entertainment Ltd.
All rights reserved.

Set in Bembo Regular
Printed in Great Britain by Clays Ltd, St Ives plc

British Library Cataloguing in Publication Data
A CIP catalogue record for this book is available from the British Library

ISBN: 978-0-141-35213-8

MIX
From responsible
sources
FSC FSC™C018179

ANGRY BIRDS™

TREASURE ISLAND

Contents

1 Pigs Ahoy!   1

2 The Old Sea Eagle   17

3 Pew and Stinky   29

4 Captain Featherbeard's Map   40

5 Long John Smooth Cheeks   55

6 All at Sea   68

7 The Octopig   79

8 Easter Egg Island   89

9 Ben Hamm   103

10 The Plan   114

11 X Marks the Spot   124

12 The Treasure   135

Contents

1

Pigs Ahoy!

One night, deep in the Bamboo Forest on the west coast of Piggy Island, three birds had been left guarding eggs. Their names were Jake, Jay and Jim and they were blue, which was lucky, because they were collectively known as the Blues.

The reason they were guarding the eggs was simple. The other inhabitants of Piggy Island, a greedy group of grunting pigs, were always trying to steal them. Why? Because their repulsive ruler, King Pig Smooth Cheeks, wanted to eat the eggs. They could be poached, scrambled, fried or boiled for all he cared, as long as they were in his belly. In days gone by there had been hundreds of eggs for the pigs to pilfer. Now there were just a few left and it was up to the Angry Birds, who included Jake, Jay and Jim, to guard them.

The Blues knew their job was important, but they didn't enjoy it. As the youngest members of the Flock they were always bursting with energy, ready to fly into action at the drop of a feather, which is why they found standing still so boring.

'This is so boring,' said Jake.

'I'm finding it much more boring than you,' sighed Jay, much to Jim's annoyance.

'Don't be a birdbrain!' said Jim. 'I'm more bored than either of you.'

The Blues were always squabbling. They'd bickered from the moment they hatched – probably even before that.

But the Blues' argument wasn't the only sound in the forest. As they quarrelled, other voices drifted through the bamboo trees:

'Yo ho ho and a barrel of grass,
Snout and crossbones on our mast . . .'

'Wait,' said Jim. 'Did you hear that?'

'Hear what?' asked Jay, keen to get back to the matter at hand.

'Someone singing!' Jim replied.

'It's probably Matilda,' Jake said, 'she's always clucking away to herself, that one.'

Matilda was another member of the Flock, a big white bird who constantly mothered the Blues, much to their embarrassment.

'I don't think so,' said Jim. It sounded a bit more . . . grunty!'

'You probably imagined it,' said Jay, dismissively.

'Did not!'

'Did too!'

'Did not!'

'Did too!'

'Yo ho ho and a barrel of grass,
Steal the eggs and steal them fast!'

'I heard it that time!' Jake yelled, spinning around. 'But where's it coming from?'

'Over there!' shouted Jim, spotting something in the trees. 'Look!'

The other two Blues followed his gaze and saw three sinister shapes silhouetted against the moon. Three pig shapes, wearing three-pointed hats.

Jay's beak drew back in a snarl. 'Pigs,' he said.

'They're after the eggs!' said Jake, glaring at the shadowy swine.

'Not a chance!' Jim yelled, leaping forward without a second thought. 'It's pig-popping time!'

The Blues may squabble but they always stick together. Jay and Jake joined the charge, ready to plough into the pigs. They were so angry that they completely forgot about the eggs they were supposed to be protecting.

Meanwhile, the pigs didn't even seem to react. They just stood there as if they wanted to be pecked.

'Stay away from our . . . OW!' said Jay as he slammed into something hard.

'Ouch!' cried Jake, as he bounced back. 'What's going on?'

'I don't know,' admitted Jim, his little head spinning. 'I thought pigs were plump and squishy, not hard and flat?

Jay gasped. 'Guys, look! These aren't real pigs.'

Jake's eyes went wide. Jay was right. They'd barrelled straight into wooden dummies – the remnants of King Pig's last Ham-o-ween party. The manic monarch had come dressed as a pirate and demanded decorations to match.

'These porkers are phoneys. Complete and utter fakes.'

'So who was snorting that song?' Jay asked.

'Them!' Jim said, turning round just in time to see a bunch of very real piggies making off with the eggs!

'It was a trick,' said Jake, 'and we fell for it.'

'Don't blame me,' said Jay, 'Jim told us to pulverize the pretend pirates!'

'No I didn't,' huffed Jim, before realizing that arguing again was the last thing they should be doing.

'THEY'RE GETTING AWAY!' they all shouted together.

The brothers flapped after the egg-pinching pigs.

'It's no use,' Jay puffed. 'They're too far now.'

'We'll never catch them,' agreed Jake. 'Red is going to go crazy when he finds out!'

Red was the leader of the Flock and the angriest bird of them all. Jim shot a disparaging look at his brother. 'Don't be such a chicken!'

Jake glanced up, noticing something in the sky. 'I'm not,' he said. 'But she is! Look!'

A shadow passed over the forest.

'Leave. Those. Eggs. Alone!' Matilda bellowed, swooping down over the swine. The hurrying hogs whimpered as she plummeted towards them, a large frying pan held high over her head.

CRASH!

She smashed the pan into the ground, sending shockwaves shooting in every direction.

The pigs were thrown one way, the eggs they'd stolen the other. Instinctively, the Blues scattered and caught the falling eggs before they could smash on the ground.

The Blues cheered. The eggs were saved. The only things that had been scrambled were the pigs themselves. Dazed and confused they tottered off to the hills, eyes still spinning from the panning they'd received. Job done!

But Matilda looked cross.

When the eggs were safely back in the nest, the large white bird turned on the Blues.

'What were you thinking?' she clucked. 'Guarding the nest is no joke! This is so typical of you three. Always running off like a bunch of birdbrains, getting yourself in trouble.'

'We're not,' huffed Jake.

'Really?' said Matilda. 'What about last week?'

The Blues looked at each other blankly.

'When you put pepper in Bomb's birdseed?' Matilda prompted.

'Oh that,' sniggered Jim. Bomb was one of their best friends, a beefy blackbird with an explosive temper. Literally explosive. While most folk blew their top when miffed, Bomb actually blew up. It was a handy trick when trying to demolish piggy forts, but not so good when he couldn't control it. Like when he was surprised. Or when he sneezed.

'Do you remember?' Jim said, trying not to giggle. 'He shoved his beak in the birdseed and –' Jim pretended to be trying not to sneeze. 'Atch – atch – atch –'

'BOOM!' the three chicks cheered, rolling about in laughter.

'It was hilarious,' Jake argued, tears rolling down his cheeks. 'Even Bomb found it funny!'

'Red didn't,' Matilda pointed out. 'Especially when the explosions nearly caused a landslide . . .'

'Oh yeah,' Jay said, meekly, recalling how the joke had ended. 'And nearly buried the eggs.'

'They were saved, though,' pointed out Jake. 'Hal got them out in time.' Hal was another member of the Flock, a green bird with an enormous beak that could fly through the air like a boomerang. He'd just managed to get the eggs away before they were crushed.

'That's not the point,' snapped Matilda. 'It's like when you glued Chuck to his perch when he was asleep.'

'Oh, he totally deserved that,' said Jim. The Blues had overheard Chuck boasting to Stella, another girl in the Flock, that he could outrun any bird on the island. Yes, it was true. Chuck was faster than any of the other birds, but there was no need for him to show off about it. The Blues slowed him down by smothering the branches of his favourite tree with the lumpy old porridge Matilda had made them for breakfast. Chuck had settled down for a nice nap and when he'd woken up (helped by a fake cry of 'Look out! Pigs!' from the Blues) he'd found himself stuck fast. He wasn't so fast any more.

'It doesn't matter whether Chuck deserved it

or not,' said Matilda. 'What if the pigs had tried to steal the eggs while we were trying to get him unstuck?'

'We would have stopped them,' insisted Jay, 'like we did today!'

'Today?' Matilda said, her voice getting shriller by the second. 'If you'd thought for a minute, rather than just charging in head first, those pigs wouldn't have been able to make off with the eggs in the first place! What if I hadn't been here? What would have happened then?'

Jim looked down, unable to meet her furious gaze. 'We would have lost the eggs.'

'Exactly.'

Silence fell as the Blues shuffled uncomfortably.

'We're sorry,' Jay said. 'It's just so dull, standing around the nest all day.'

Jake nodded. 'We want adventures.'

Jim beamed at the word. 'Excitement,' he added.

Matilda glanced over towards the broken

pirate-pig dummies.

'Adventure, eh?' she said, a smile spreading over her beak. 'You know, there's a story I was told when I was a chick . . .'

'Is it exciting?' Jay's eyes were wide, and he was hanging on Matilda's every word.

Matilda grinned. 'Oh yes!'

'Are there pirates?' Jake asked.

'The worst pirates in history,' Matilda said.

Jim's eyes went wide. 'What about monsters? I love monsters!'

Matilda loomed over the small chicks. 'There are monsters and mermaids and, best of all . . .'

'What?' the Blues cried in unison.

Matilda's eyes narrowed. 'Lost treasure, buried beneath the sand! Would you like to hear the story?'

'YES!' Jay, Jake and Jim yelled, jumping up and down around the nest.

'Then I shall begin.' Matilda settled back and started her tale. 'It all happened on an island, much like this one, long, long ago . . .'

Dramatis personæ

Billy Beak
– Mighty Eagle

Jake, Jay and Jim Hawkins
– The Blues

Captain Speedster
– Chuck

The crew – Bomb, Hal,
Stella and Terence

Dr Matilda
– Matilda

Squire Red
– Red

Pew
– Corporal Pig

Stinky
– Foreman Pig

Long John Smooth Cheeks
– King Pig

The crew of the Hogspignola
– Minion Pigs

The Octopig
– Himself

Ben Hamm –
Professor Pig

2

The Old Sea Eagle

'Jim, wake up.'

Jim Hawkins groaned in his sleep. He was in the middle of a dream. His favourite dream of all.

He was a ship's captain, with the sea breeze rushing through his feathers. He was on a treasure hunt, searching for lost gold. Troubled waters lay ahead, but Captain Jim didn't care. He laughed in the face of danger, stuck his tongue out at peril and blew raspberries in the general direction of fear. He would fight the monsters, find the treasure and . . .

'Wake up, wake up!'

'W-what is it?' Jim groaned, his feathered face creasing into a frown.

'We've got to do our chores,' replied the excited voice. 'Come on. Up and at them.'

'You've got to be kidding,' Jim opened one eye and sighed. No, they weren't. In front of him, his two brothers – Jay and Jake – were bouncing up and down with glee.

They'd lived all their young lives in the same small nest, nestled into a cliff, overlooking the ocean. Jim liked it here. Why wouldn't he? They awoke every morning with the smell of the salty sea in their nostrils, the sound of the waves crashing into the rocks below in their ears. They could gaze out from their beds, watching ships sail majestically across the horizon.

But that was the problem. Jim wanted to be on one of those ships, not stuck here in this poky little nest. He wanted a life of adventure. Hoisting the rigging and splicing the mainsail. Or was it splicing the rigging and hoisting the mainsail? Jim didn't know, and that was the point. He wanted to learn. He wanted to be a sailor, but

above everything else he wanted to be a captain.

'We need to gather fresh sticks for the nest,' said Jay, snapping Jim's thoughts back to the here and now.

'And make sure there's enough grain,' added Jake.

This didn't make sense. His brothers hated having to help around the place. He did too. Nest-work was so boring.

'What's the rush?'

'It's Saturday,' Jay said, trying to nudge him out of his bed of twigs.

'So?'

Jake pecked at him from the other side. 'The day we go to see Billy Beak, remember?'

'As long as we do our chores,' Jay nodded.

Finally, Jim started paying attention. Billy Beak!

'Why didn't you say so?' he chirped, bounding out of the nest. 'Come on, we've got sticks to find.'

Billy Beak lived in a damp and somewhat spooky cave in a remote part of Birdie Island. Most folk gave him a wide berth – probably because he was extremely grumpy and more than a little rude. All Billy wanted was to be left alone. Woe betide anyone who wandered too close to his cave –

they soon felt the sharp end of his beak.

Not the Hawkins brothers. They loved Billy. In fact, the old hermit was their biggest hero. Literally. Billy Beak was the largest eagle you've ever seen. Absolutely massive. Which was another reason why most birds were scared of him. The Hawkinses had been warned against disturbing Billy from the day they'd hatched.

As with most things in life, the Hawkinses ignored this advice, and for a very good reason. Billy told the best stories about life on the open sea. Long ago, the eagle had been a sailor. He had travelled far and wide, seeing things that other birds could only dream about. He was also surprisingly fond of the Hawkins brothers. They were the only birds he tolerated, and he would thrill them every Saturday night with swashbuckling sagas and terrifying tales.

This evening was no different.

'And you defeated the ferocious Octopig on your own?' repeated Jim, eyes wide as Billy

finished yet another of his stories.

'And found the lost city of Piglantis?' gasped Jay, staring up at the enormous bird.

'With its mountains of glittering gems?' whispered an awestruck Jake.

Billy's massive beak creaked as he smiled. 'And all before breakfast,' he boomed.

'WOW!' said the Hawkinses in unison.

Billy yawned and began to rub his eyes.

'Can you tell us another?' asked Jim hopefully.

'Another! Another! Another!' chanted his brothers.

'In a minute,' Billy rumbled, his hooded eyes closing. 'This old sea bird needs forty winks. Telling stories is exhausting, you know, especially when you get to my age.'

'Awwwww,' complained Jim, but Billy was already asleep.

'That was brilliant,' Jay said, hopping into the mouth of the cave. It was starting to rain and he didn't want to get wet.

'He'll tell us another after his nap,' said Jake. 'He always does, isn't that right, Jim?'

Jim didn't answer. He was peering inside the cave, right into the shadows. 'What's that?'

'What's what?'

Jim ventured a bit further in. 'Over here. It looks like a chest.'

Sure enough, at the very back of Billy Beak's cave, was a chest, its metal hinges tarnished and rusty.

'Perhaps it's a treasure chest,' said Jake.

'From Piglantis?' Jay asked excitedly.

'There's only one way to find out,' said Jake.

'We have to open it,' said Jay.

Jim shook his head. 'We can't. Billy won't like it.'

'He won't know,' Jay insisted, sneaking a sly glance back at the snoozing eagle. 'He's asleep.'

Jim sighed. Perhaps it wouldn't hurt to have a quick peek. He bounced forward and pecked at the heavy-looking padlock. 'We'll never get that open,' he said, glumly, 'not without the key.'

'Who needs a key when you've got this!' Jim

and Jay turned to see Jake clutching a crowbar he'd found underneath a pile of tin cans. 'Stand aside, feather-brains, and watch a master at work.'

Even Jay wasn't sure about this. 'I don't know,' he said quietly, as Jake struggled to push the crowbar under the lid of the chest. 'It doesn't feel right.'

'Don't be such a scaredy chick,' Jake hissed, as the crowbar slipped into place. 'Was Billy scared when he faced the slimy tentacles of the evil Octopig? No. Did he wonder if he was doing the right thing when he fought phantom merhogs in the haunted shipwreck? Not on your nelly.'

The crowbar started to bend as Jake heaved.

'I don't think this is the same thing,' said Jim.

'Oh, shut your beak and lend a wing,' Jake responded.

Jim rolled his eyes but did what he was told, helping Jake bend the crowbar back. The lid still wouldn't budge.

'You two are rubbish,' said Jay, jumping in the air. 'Here, do it like this.'

The move didn't go as Jay had planned. He crashed down on the crowbar, which bent under his weight before snapping back like a spring. The three birds were catapulted into the air.

'Waaaah!' they yelled together as they bounced off stalactites and ricocheted from stalagmites. Although that wasn't the worst of it. With a thud, Jim slammed into Billy!

The eagle awoke with a squawk, before glaring down at the upended chest on the cave floor. The lid was still firmly shut, but the crowbar was sticking out at an awkward angle.

'This isn't what it looks like,' Jake said quickly.

'We just wanted to see what was inside,' added Jay.

Billy glared at them, his bloodshot eyes bulging in their baggy sockets. His feathers bristled and his beak curled into a snarl.

'Get out!' he growled.

'We're sorry,' sniffed Jim, tears pricking his eyes. 'Really, really sorry.'

Billy Beak exploded in fury.

'Get out,' he shouted in a roar that sounded like a thousand thunderstorms rolled into one. 'Get out! Get out! GET OUT!!!'

3

Pew and Stinky

The Hawkinses bolted from Billy's cave and half flew down the mountainside. Behind them they could still hear Billy roaring in anger.

'I told you we shouldn't have tried to open it,' gasped Jake, as they eventually came to a halt by the edge of a wood.

'You what?' said Jim, hardly believing his ears.

'And I said it was a stupid idea from the beginning,' Jay added, giving Jim a glare.

'Yeah,' said Jake, shaking his head in disgust. 'I don't know why we let you talk us into it, Jim.'

'But I didn't . . .' Jim stammered, gaping at Jay. 'You said . . .'

'Oh, that's how it is, is it?' said Jake. 'He's going to try to blame us!'

With that, the Hawkins brothers started bickering. Before too long the squabble had turned into a quarrel and the quarrel turned into a full-blown row. The three birds bounced up and down in frustration, chirping furiously and trying their hardest to drown each other out.

'Oh dear, oh dear, oh dear,' came a voice from behind them.

The Hawkinses span around and stared into the trees. The sun had set and it was hard to make anything out in the half-light.

'Who's there?' called Jim, his brothers shifting to stand beak-by-beak beside him.

'What have we here, Pew?' said a big, bulky figure striding through the trees. It was a bird, or at least the Hawkinses thought it was. It had a long tapered beak that jutted out over a big, bushy moustache and one of its wild eyes was covered by a black eye-patch. On the top of its green head it wore a tatty three-sided hat and it smelled. Bad.

'I don't know, Stinky.' A slightly smaller emerald-green bird stepped out from behind the first. This one had a similar, if slightly wonky, beak and wore a brightly coloured bandana over some sort of helmet. 'Three little tweets having a right old ding-dong.'

The smaller newcomer's eye-patch flipped up

to reveal a perfectly healthy eye. His pink tongue flicked in and out of his toothy mouth almost instantaneously.

'Who are you?' demanded Jim, who thought he knew almost everyone on Birdie Island.

'Us?' replied the larger of the two. 'Why we're just two sailors making our way to the docks.'

The Hawkinses stared.

'Sailors?'

'That's us,' grinned the bigger bird from beneath his moustache. 'I'm Stinky.'

'And I'm Pew,' said the smaller one.

'Wow,' said Jay. 'Real-life sailors.'

'We want to be sailors,' admitted Jake.

Jim nodded. 'You're the only ones we've met.'

'Except for old Billy,' Jay pointed out, drooping as he remembered how much they'd upset their old friend.

Stinky gasped. 'Billy?' he asked in a hushed voice.

Pew raised his eyebrows, sending his eye-patch snapping up again. 'Not Billy Beak?'

Now it was Jim's turn to look astonished. 'You know him?'

'Know him?' Stinky repeated. 'Everybody knows him. He's the most famous sea bird of all time.'

'He fought the phantom merhogs of the haunted shipwreck,' Pew said, adjusting his eye-patch.

'That's right,' said Jay. 'And defeated the ferocious Octopig.'

'He's a legend,' Stinky told them.

'We know,' Jake said, his feathers bristling with pride. 'He's our friend.'

'No way,' gasped Pew.

Jim shuffled uncomfortably. 'At least he was . . .'

Stinky shuffled nearer. 'What happened, little fellow?'

The Hawkinses told the sailors about the treasure chest and the crowbar and being chucked out of Billy's cave.

Pew tut-tutted. 'A sorry tale,' he murmured.

'But perhaps we can help,' said Stinky, winking

at his bandana-wearing buddy.

'How?' asked Jake, hope creeping back into his voice.

Stinky leaned in conspiratorially. 'It's a well known fact that Billy Beak likes sardines.'

'Is it?' asked Jay.

'Tinned sardines,' said Pew. 'Loves 'em. Can't get enough.'

'I would think that if someone offered him a tin of sardines, Billy would forgive them anything,' Stinky suggested.

Jim's heart sank. 'But we don't have a tin of sardines.'

'Don't you?' said Pew, nudging Stinky, who promptly produced a tin from behind his chubby back.

'You do now,' said Stinky.

The Hawkinses bounced up and down on the spot.

'Can we have it? Can we have it? Can we have it?' they chirped excitedly.

'What's the magic word?' asked Stinky.

'Pleeeeeease,' the birds offered as one, cheering as the sailor tossed the tin towards them.

'Well, what are you waiting for, mates?' said Pew. 'Go and give it to the old freak.'

Stinky nudged the smaller sailor in the ribs.

'Er, I mean, legend,' Pew corrected himself.

Chirping their thanks, the birds set off up the path.

Behind them, Pew grunted happily at Stinky.

'It worked,' he said, grinning a horrible grin.

'Of course it did,' said Stinky, scratching under his beak with his tongue. 'And good job too. These false beaks are as itchy as anything. Oink.'

The moon came out from behind a cloud and at that moment the sailors noticed the Hawkinses had stopped and were looking at them curiously. They both grinned sheepishly, Stinky's cardboard beak snapping back over his snout.

'Just one thing?' said Jim, his eyes narrowing.

'Y-y-yes, matey?' enquired Pew.

'Why are you green?' asked Jay.

Pew's smile faltered. 'We, er, we . . .'

'Get seasick,' cut in Stinky quickly.

'That's it,' nodded Pew. 'As a parrot.'

The Hawkinses gave the two sailors a long, hard look – and then shrugged.

'Fair enough,' said Jake and the birds continued on their way. 'Goodnight!'

'Phew,' said Pew as soon as the Hawkinses were out of earshot. 'That was close.'

But Stinky was already trudging after them. 'Come on,' he called over his shoulder. 'We haven't any time to lose.'

'Billy,' Jake called, as they approached the cave. 'It's us. We've got something for you.'

'Go away,' the eagle growled. 'I'm not home.'

They could see the tip of Billy's beak sticking out of the entrance.

'But we've got a present for you,' said Jake,

nudging Jim forward. 'To say sorry!'

'Don't like presents,' Billy snarled, his beak disappearing further into the shadows. 'Leave me alone.'

'Maybe we should open it,' Jay suggested. 'Let him smell the sardines.'

'Sardines?' Billy said eagerly, his beak already watering. 'Did you say sardines?'

Jim grinned. 'Yes, Billy. Two nice, and in no way suspicious-looking, sailors gave us a tin. We wonder if you'd like to –'

'What are you doing?' Billy shouted and swooped out of the cave. The Hawkinses gave a surprised chirp. They'd never seen Billy fly. He soared straight up into the night sky and performed a perfect loop-the-loop.

'Amazing,' said Jay, grinning wildly.

'Ooh, he's doing another one,' said Jake, gasping in awe.

'And he's heading straight for us!' gulped Jim.

Billy Beak thundered towards them, his hungry

eyes fixed on the little tin of sardines.

'Ruuuuuuuuuuuuun!' shouted Jim, as he threw the tin high into the air. Billy snapped his beak around the tin without even stopping, ploughing straight into the ground.

Mud, feathers and even the odd tree flew into the air. The brothers closed their eyes tight. It was as if the sky had landed on their heads.

And then it was all over. The dust settled, along with a number of large boulders. The blue birds lay panting in a newly created crater, with Billy slumped to the side with a satisfied smile plastered across his beak.

'I love sardines,' he admitted. 'Thank you, boys.'

'Don't thank us,' muttered Jim, trying to work out which way up the world should be. 'Thank Pew and Stinky.'

'Who?' asked Bill.

'The sea birds who ... gave us ... the tin,' Jake panted.

'Never heard of them,' said Billy.

'That's them there actually,' said Jay, pointing towards two green sailors scurrying off with a battered box. 'Those two running back down the hill with your old treasure chest.'

It took a second for Jay's words to sink in, but when they did all four birds shouted in unison: 'THEY'VE STOLEN THE CHEST!'

4

Captain Featherbeard's Map

The birds had been tricked. Pew and Stinky had only wanted to nab Billy Beak's chest. The other problem was that they were now so dazed by being caught in one of Billy's feeding frenzies that they couldn't give chase. Billy was the same. He said he was stuffed to the eyebrows with sardines, which was odd, as it was a very small tin for such a big bird. But he'd never had much of an appetite.

As for Pew and Stinky, the two pigs – for that's what they were – had made it safely to the beach where an extremely large and bulky contraption was waiting for them.

'There it is, Pew,' said Stinky, proudly. 'My

official steam-powered, reinforced piggy chest-smash-a-tron. Designed it myself. Oink!'

The two pigs slid the chest under the giant mallet at the bottom of the shonky looking device. Pew noticed that the padlock had sprung off.

'Oh, look,' he said, absently. 'That must have happened when we stole it.'

'Never mind that,' said Stinky, checking that the machine was in working order. 'We need to smash the chest open to get the map.'

'The map?' asked Pew, his eye-patch springing up again.

'The map in the chest,' Stinky spluttered. 'The reason we've gone to all this trouble. The reason we tricked those stupid birds. The reason I built the official steam-powered, reinforced piggy chest-smash-a-tron.'

Pew looked confused.

'The treasure map, you gammon-headed twit!' Stinky exploded, jumping over to the machine's controls.

'Oh yeah,' smiled Pew, finally remembering. 'But now that the lock's broken . . .'

'I haven't got time for that now,' yelled Stinky, as his contraption started to clunk into life. 'I've got to open that lid.'

'Fair enough,' said Pew, although Stinky couldn't hear him. The chest-smash-a-tron was shuddering, its wooden gears grinding, pistons pumping and steam hissing from every joint. Slowly the hammer started to rise up above Billy Beak's chest, ready to break it open.

'Is it supposed to be making that much noise?' called Pew warily, as the entire structure began to judder.

'Eh?' asked Stinky, as each and every safety valve shattered.

'I said, is it supposed to sound like that?' shouted Pew, as springs started pinging off in all directions.

'What?' hollered Stinky, ducking as a flying cog nearly sliced him in two.

'I said . . .'

But Pew never finished his sentence. Instead he squealed at the top of his voice as the official steam-powered, reinforced piggy chest-smash-a-tron exploded into tiny little pieces.

When the smoke cleared, the two seriously singed swine blinked at the wreckage. The chest-smash-a-tron was scattered all over the beach. Billy's treasure chest, on the other hand, was where it had been all along, still in one piece.

Stinky looked like he might cry.

'Don't worry,' said Pew, leaping over to the crate. 'It wasn't locked anyway.'

With a flick of his snout, the pig knocked the lid of the chest open.

Stinky immediately forgot his disappointment. 'The map,' he gabbled. 'Let me see. Let me see!'

The two pigs looked into the chest and their jaws hit the ground.

Billy Beak's chest was empty.

'Nooooooooooooo!' wailed the pigs.

'Don't worry,' said Billy Beak. 'The chest's empty.'

The Hawkinses looked at each other in amazement.

'But . . .' said Jim.

'But . . .' said Jay.

'But . . .' said Jake.

Billy nodded. 'You're probably wondering why I chucked you out of the cave for trying to open it, aren't you?'

The Hawkinses nodded.

Billy sniffed, looking a bit embarrassed. 'Force of habit. Sorry. I used to keep something pretty important in there.'

'The lost treasures of Piglantis?' Jay asked.

'Instructions for how to defeat the Octopig?' Jake asked.

'More sardines?' Jim asked.

'More important than all of those put together,' said Billy, trying to lean in closer, which was tricky as he was so big and they were so small. 'Captain Featherbeard's secret map.'

'Oooooooh,' said the Hawkinses.

'You don't know what that is, do you?' said Billy.

'No,' they admitted.

'Captain Featherbeard was the finest captain I ever had,' Billy admitted. 'And long ago, he gave me the secret map to his secret stash of top-secret eggs.'

'Secret eggs,' the brothers repeated in awe.

Billy nodded. 'They're the rarest eggs in the world. Laid by the ancient and now extinct What's-their-name Birds of Forgotten Island.'

'Where's that?'

Billy shook his head. 'Can't remember. All I know is that they are said to be the eggiest eggs ever. The whitest shells. The perfect shape. If you know your eggs these are the best. Absolutely priceless.'

'But if you know where they are buried, why don't you go and dig them up?' asked Jim.

'Oh, I'm too long in the beak for all that

adventuring stuff,' Billy told them. 'Treasure hunting's a game for young chicks not old birds like me.'

'We're young chicks,' piped up Jay. 'We could find 'em?'

'No!' Billy barked. 'I promised the Captain I'd keep the map safe so that no pigs could get their stinking little trotters on the eggs. That's the real reason I stopped sailoring and retired here to this cave. There are too many pirate pigs on the open seas nowadays, and if the pigs find the map and then those eggs, well, they'd just gobble them up. Captain Featherbeard's treasure would be lost forever.'

'But why did you take the map from the chest?' Jim asked.

'Just in case some pigs disguised themselves as birds and tried to distract me with a tin of sardines so they could steal it.'

'Yeah, like that happens often,' scoffed Jay.

'So, where is it?' asked Jake.

'Erm,' Billy said, trying to remember. 'Oh yes.

I popped it under a flower pot in the main town square.'

'What?' the brothers said at once.

'Hmmmm,' Billy considered. 'Perhaps that wasn't the safest place. Can you fetch it for me?'

'Us?' Jake squeaked. 'Fetch a real-life treasure map?'

Billy nodded, nearly flattening them with his giant beak.

'Yes, as long as you promise me one thing.'

'Anything,' said Jay.

'I made a pledge to the Captain. Those eggs must stay where they are. Promise me that you'll bring the map straight back here. Do not decide to go and find the treasure yourself. It's far too dangerous.'

The Hawkinses gasped at the very thought.

'You can trust us,' said Jim.

'Good,' said Billy, smiling proudly.

'You know,' said Jake, after they had recovered the secret map to Captain Featherbeard's secret stash of top-secret eggs from beneath the flower pot, 'we could just go and find the treasure ourselves.'

Jim wrinkled his beak. 'Does anyone remember promising not to do exactly that?' he asked.

'Nope,' said the other two, distracted by the yellowed scroll.

'That's all right, then,' said Jim with a grin. 'So where do we start?'

'First things first,' Jake said, rolling the map out on the grass. On it was a faded drawing of an island shaped like a great big egg. 'We can't tell anyone that we've got the map to Captain Featherbeard's treasure.'

'Isn't that the map to Captain Featherbeard's treasure?' said a familiar voice. Groaning, the brothers looked up to see Dr Matilda, the local quack, standing over them.

'Nope,' said Jim, quickly. 'Don't think so.'

'Squire Red,' Dr Matilda called to a passing

dignitary in a rather splendid hat. 'These young chicks have found the map to Captain Featherbeard's treasure!'

'We really haven't,' Jay lied, trying to place himself between the map and the rapidly approaching bird.

'Caw!' said the Squire. 'That's the fabled Easter Egg Island.'

'Easter Egg Island?' asked Jake. 'Isn't it supposed to be haunted?'

'Don't be daft,' said Jim, who was more worried about how fast everything was escalating. 'There's no such thing as ghosts.'

'Exactly,' agreed Squire Red. 'Captain Featherbeard's treasure, eh? The rarest eggs in the world.'

'Absolutely priceless,' said Dr Matilda. 'I thought they were lost forever.'

'Me too! Where did you get the map, lads?' the Squire asked.

'Billy Beak sent us to get it,' Jay blurted out.

'Billy Beak?' repeated the Squire. 'That old rogue. I should have known it. Up there in his cave, too good for the rest of us. Typical that he'd try to keep this to himself. Well, that settles it. We must mount an expedition.'

'A treasure hunt,' clucked Dr Matilda, bouncing up and down. 'How thrilling.'

This was getting out of control. The trouble with Squire Red was that he always thought he knew best – even when he plainly didn't. Once his mind was made up there was no changing it.

Jake thought he'd give it a try anyway. 'Shouldn't we ask Billy?' he said innocently.

'To lead the expedition?' the Squire spluttered. 'No, no, no! Beak's a has-been. We need someone who knows the seven seas like the back of his plumage. Don't worry, boys, I know the perfect bird, the finest captain on these shores.'

'You know, I think we did promise not to look for the treasure,' protested Jim, but of course it was too late. Dr Matilda was so excited that she threw the dainty parasol she was carrying in the air.

As it soared upward it accidentally popped a balloon that was suspending a pirate pig cunningly disguised as a cloud.

The spying swine wailed as it tumbled from the sky to land beside two very familiar figures.

'Well,' said Stinky. 'What did you find out?'

'Never float above a bird holding a dainty parasol?' said the pirate pig, its eyes rolling.

'About the treasure!' snapped Pew.

'Oh, that,' answered the pig. 'Nothing much, other than the fact that they've found Captain Featherbeard's map . . .'

5

Long John Smooth Cheeks

Squire Red was as good as his word. As soon as he'd got over the shock that the secret map to Captain Featherbeard's secret stash of top-secret eggs had been discovered, he'd hired the best sea captain he could find.

Unfortunately, as the birds of Birdie Island are known to be notoriously bad sailors, he didn't have much in the way of choice.

In fact, there was only one choice.

Captain Speedster was a bright yellow bird who lived up to his name. He dashed here, there and everywhere as he tried to pull together a crew for their expedition.

Before too long he had found everyone he

needed and lined them up on the quayside. There was a pink bird called Miss Stella, a large black bird called Mr Bomb, a bird with a massive beak called Mr Hal and a huge bird called Mr Terence. Seriously, Mr Terence was gigantic. Not as big as Billy Beak, but larger than the rest of the birds put together.

'A fine-looking crew,' Squire Red said, as Captain Speedster beamed with pride. 'I'm sure they'll be a credit to your ship.'

The Captain's beak fell. 'Ship, sir?' he said, looking a bit confused.

Jim started to feel uneasy. 'You do have a ship, don't you, Captain?'

Captain Speedster snorted with laughter. 'Of course not! What would I need with a ship?'

Dr Matilda looked dumbstruck. 'You're a sea captain!'

'I am, yes,' nodded Speedster, happily.

'Without a ship?' Jay spluttered.

'So how are we going to sail to Easter Egg Island?' Jake asked.

'Oh, yeah,' said Speedster, smiling sheepishly at the Squire who was getting more red-feathered by the second. 'I can see how that might cause a problem.'

Dr Matilda shuffled forward, trying to defuse the situation. Squire Red had a bit of a temper. 'I'm sure there's a simple solution to all of this. Why don't we –'

'SOMEONE BUILD ME A SHIP!' bellowed the Squire. 'NOW!'

Speedster's crew tried to do just that. They tried very hard. In fact, after four days of work, they'd managed to construct something resembling a ship, but only just.

Its sails pointed down instead of up.

It had huge holes in the hull, which, according to Captain Speedster, would help let water out.

Worst of all, it was moored on the top of the tallest mountain on Birdie Island, about as far away from the sea as was possible.

The birds gathered to inspect it.

'We're never going to find the treasure,' Jim said sadly.

'After treasure, is ye?' came a rough voice from behind. 'Then it looks like I arrived just in time.'

A stout stranger grinned at them, piggy eyes sparkling with mischief.

No, not piggy eyes. The stranger wasn't a pig. He didn't even have a snout. A bright yellow beak jutted out proudly above his sly mouth. OK, so the feathers on his head looked like they were stuck in a pair of wriggling pig-ears, but the beak proved it – he was a bird. A large, green bird.

'Who are you?' Jim said what everyone else was thinking.

'The name's Long John Smooth Cheeks,' the stranger announced, pushing back his shabby chef's hat with the end of a tattered crutch. 'Pleased to make yer acquaintance.'

'What do you know of treasure?' Squire Red asked suspiciously.

'Only how to finds it,' said Smooth Cheeks, his smirk growing wider still.

'You're not a sea captain, are you?' said Speedster nervously. He didn't want any competition for this job.

'Me, sir?' laughed Smooth Cheeks. 'No, I be nothing more than a humble ship's cook.'

'We do have a ship,' chipped in Dr Matilda. Smooth Cheeks looked up at the effort on the side of the mountain.

'Is that what it is?' he said, shaking his huge head. 'Looks to me like you needs a team who can builds you a ship worthy of a treasure hunt.'

'We do,' agreed the Squire. 'But where can we find such a crew on Birdie Island?'

Smooth Cheeks gasped in surprise. 'Well, blow me down. If it ain't me old crew standing right over there. It's almost as if this had been planned all along. What a coincidence!'

Sure enough, a rag-tag bunch of sailors had gathered alongside them. All of them had slightly wonky beaks.

Jake nudged Jim. 'Do those two look familiar to you?' he asked, pointing out a bird with a bushy moustache and another wearing a bandana over an oversized helmet. 'Like Pew and Stinky?' The two sailors noticed they'd been spotted and immediately swapped their eye-patches from one eye to the other.

'Nope,' Jim shrugged. 'Never seen them before in my life.'

'Could you get our craft shipshape?' asked the Squire.

Smooth Cheeks sucked air through his teeth. 'Reckon so, but it won't come cheap.'

'How much?' asked Speedster, not looking at all happy with the situation.

The large sailor-bird smirked. 'Well, I'm sure we could come to an arrangement . . .'

Before you could say, 'Hang on, aren't they just pigs disguised as birds again?' Long John Smooth Cheeks's crew had transformed Speedster's sorry excuse for a ship into the finest vessel imaginable. 'So, is ye happy?' Smooth Cheeks asked the Squire when they had managed to get the ship to shore.

Red nodded enthusiastically. 'Absolutely. You've done a wonderful job.'

'All part of the agreement, sir. We'll build ye a lovely ship . . .'

'And we let you sail it for us, yes, we know,' said Dr Matilda. 'And you're sure there's nothing else you want. Gold or gems or whatever?'

Smooth Cheeks shook his head. 'Got no need for them, Doctor. All I asks for is a kitchen to cook in and for me shipmates to steer. We're not happy unless we're at sea, see.'

Jim sniffed. 'Doesn't it sound a little too good to be true, Squire?'

The Squire nodded. 'Indeed it does. And as I

always say, "If something sounds too good to be true . . ."'

'Yes?' said Smooth Cheeks softly.

'"Agree to it immediately!"' Squire Red beamed, before his face creased in concern. 'Although there is one thing I'm not too sure about.'

Now it was the chef's turn to look worried. 'And what's that, your lordship?'

'The name,' said the Squire.

Smooth Cheeks glanced at the nameplate screwed on to the ship's hull.

'The *Hogspignola*. What be wrong with that?'

'Isn't it a little . . . piggy?' Dr Matilda asked.

'Don't thinks so,' said the cook.

'And then there's the figurehead,' said the Squire, pointing at the large wooden pig's face carved into the bow of the ship.

'Looks noble to me, it does,' insisted Smooth Cheeks.

'And in no way, you know . . . snouty?' asked Speedster.

'Maybe from this angle,' said the cook, 'but not from the front, trust me. You do trust me, don't you?'

The birds all looked at each other for a moment, before the Squire's beak broke into a smile.

'Of course we do. Come on, let's set sail.'

'Raise the anchor,' yelled Captain Speedster and the Hawkinses hoisted the winch. The heavy anchor clanked from the water, but the ship didn't budge.

'We're still too heavy,' declared Smooth Cheeks. 'Something be weighing us down.'

All eyes turned to the hulking form of Mr Terence, who glowered at them. The deck planks were beginning to buckle under his weight.

So the huge bird was rolled overboard, landing in the water with a splash, and the *Hogspignola* finally swept out of the harbour.

On the deck, Jim Hawkins watched Long John Smooth Cheeks and his snorting shipmates.

'They do look very green, don't they?' he said to Jay and Jake.

'They probably get seasick,' said Dr Matilda, bouncing past happily.

'Hmmmmm,' they wondered.

6

All at Sea

It turned out that Smooth Cheeks's shipmates really did get seasick. In fact, almost everyone on board the *Hogspignola* was soon feeling under the weather.

Their passage wasn't a smooth one. The ship bucked and tossed on the rough seas, gale-force winds blowing them this way, then that way and then back again for good measure.

After a while, all you could hear was the creaking of the timber and the groans of the crew. All except the Hawkinses that is. The blue chicks were having a whale of a time, clambering up the rigging, hoisting sails and even taking the wheel when Captain Speedster got bored of navigating (which happened approximately eight minutes into the voyage).

Jim even asked if they could swab the poop deck, but no one seemed to know where the poop deck was, although Dr Matilda thought it sounded quite rude.

The days were long and the nights stormy. Soon the birds had all but forgotten what dry land even looked like.

The ship was just as Long John Smooth Cheeks had promised. With huge billowing sails, polished timbers and plenty of portholes, no expense had been spared. Smooth Cheeks's living quarters were huge, with the finest hammocks anyone had ever seen and oodles of comfy chairs, couches and cushions. You could easily call it luxurious. Strangely, the birds were crammed into two cramped cabins that looked suspiciously like cupboards. Probably because they were cupboards.

When the birds complained, Smooth Cheeks

just produced the agreement Squire Red had signed. It said that Smooth Cheeks would get the biggest cabin and the best hammock and as many cushions as his heart desired – which seemed to be a lot! Of course, the birds had no idea if the agreement really said this or not as birds can't read, but Smooth Cheeks just reminded them of the treasure that would be theirs when they reached Easter Egg Island.

'The rarest eggs in all the world,' he said, salivating just a little. 'Just imagine.'

And so they did and forgot about their sleeping quarters for a bit – until they tried to get to sleep again, that is. Captain Speedster's snoring kept Squire Red and Dr Matilda up all night, while in the next cabin Mr Hal repeatedly poked Miss Stella in the eye with his beak every time he rolled over.

Still, the birds reasoned, at least they had a renowned ship's cook to prepare their meals.

There was, however, a slight snag.

It soon became apparent that Long John Smooth Cheeks couldn't cook for toffee, or for any other confectionary for that matter.

On the first day he served up sludgy grass biscuits. 'Ideal for dipping in tea,' he said.

'We have tea?' asked the Squire hopefully.

'No,' admitted Smooth Cheeks, 'but I could brew you some, if ye like?'

So he did. It tasted a lot like grass.

The next day he served up porridge. 'Why is it green?' the Captain asked, looking suspiciously at

the gloop in his bowl.

'That would be me secret ingredient, sir,' whispered Smooth Cheeks.

'Is the secret ingredient grass?' Jim asked.

'Yes, Jim,' grinned the cook.

'I thought you said you were a chef,' Squire Red said, pushing his bowl away.

'I am, sir. Have been since I were a piglet, er, I mean chick. Never 'ad any complaints about me grub. Do ye want to see me references again?'

He produced a scroll, full of scrawled writing, not that the Squire could read a word.

'It's all here, sir,' Smooth Cheeks said. 'Every ship I've ever served on. The *Sea Snout*. The *Flying Sow*. The *Black Boar*.'

Dr Matilda narrowed her eyes. 'They're all a bit piggish, aren't they?'

'I don't thinks so,' the cook insisted, distracting the birds by shoving a cauldron of his foul-smelling slop under their noses. 'Anyway, who's for seconds?'

It continued this way for weeks. Smooth Cheeks served up grass stew, grass soup, grass goulash, grass pancakes, grass curry and, as a special treat on the Squire's birthday, grass ice cream sundaes (with special grass sauce).

'Couldn't we have something different tomorrow?' asked Jay one evening, as he finished his plate of grass on toast (without the toast).

Smooth Cheeks's bulging eyes lit up. 'Well, if you birds could spare me an egg, I could whip up an omelette in no time.'

'What?' exclaimed Squire Red, his right eye twitching in outrage. 'Eat eggs? Birds don't eat eggs! It's out of the question!'

'Of course,' Smooth Cheeks muttered, backtracking quickly. 'What a silly thing for an old sea bird like me to suggest. A thousand apologies, your Squire-ness.'

'Besides,' moaned Jim, 'we haven't got any even if we wanted some. That's why we're searching for Captain Featherbeard's treasure.'

The chef glowered at the young chick. 'Grass surprise it be tomorrow, then.'

'What's the surprise?' Jake asked, already fearing the worse.

'It's made of grass,' explained the fuzzy-faced sailor who looked suspiciously like Stinky as he helped Smooth Cheeks clear the tables.

So the voyage continued, each crew member scanning the horizon for the fabled Easter Egg Island.

Every day was the same – except for one that was very, very different.

It began the same as normal. Jim, Jake and Jay had skipped their breakfast of scrambled grass and were up in the crow's nest looking for signs of land. As usual, all they could see were miles and miles of choppy sea.

Down below, on the deck, Smooth Cheeks's crew were singing an old sea shanty.

'Yo ho ho and a barrel of grass,
Snout and crossbones on our mast.

Yo ho ho and a barrel of grass,
Steal the eggs and steal them fast!'

The Hawkinses were humming along, without really paying attention to the lyrics, before they realized they could hear another noise. A low, rumbling snort.

Jake leaned out of the crow's nest, straining to listen. 'What is that?'

'Don't know,' said Jay, 'but it sounds like it's coming from beneath the ship.'

Jim gave his brothers a look. 'Under the water? But that makes no sense.'

The others had heard it too. Down on the deck the Squire popped out of the cabin-cupboard to see what the racket was. Even the crew stopped singing – except for the sailor that looked suspiciously like Pew, who carried on at the top of his grating voice.

'Yo ho ho and a barrel of grass . . .'

'It's getting louder,' Jim said nervously, as the rumbling got deeper. It seemed closer.

'Snout and crossbones on our mast . . .'

'The ship's starting to shake,' said Jay, holding on to the mast.

'Yo ho ho and a barrel of grass . . .'

'Look at the water,' shouted Jake. All around the Hogspignola the surface of the sea was a broiling mass of foam, as if something was rushing up to meet them. Something from the depths below.

'Steal the eggs and steal them fa—'

With a deafening crash, eight gigantic columns erupted from the churning waters. They were a sickly yellow-green colour and each column was

lined with what looked like giant suckers.

Jim's suddenly realized what they were looking at.

'Tentacles!' he yelled, trying to stop himself being thrown out of the now violently shaking crow's nest. 'They're giant tentacles!'

The creature began to wrap its tentacles around the ship. Then a gargantuan green head emerged. It had colossal eyes and a stubby snout that blew jets of water high into the air, and it smelled of something very, very rotten.

'Could it be . . . ?' Jake started.

'YES!' screamed Jim. 'It's the ferocious OCTOPIG!'

'And it looks hungry . . .' whimpered Jake.

7

The Octopig

Jake was right. The Octopig was hungry. In fact, it was absolutely starving. It hadn't eaten a ship in weeks. Not even a small one. With a deafening roar it plucked the *Hogspignola* from the ocean, its goofy teeth glinting in the sunlight.

Below, Long John Smooth Cheeks came blundering out of the galley, eyes wide as he took in the monstrous beast.

'What are ye waiting for, ye lily-livered layabouts?' he yelled at his sea birds. 'ATTACK!'

In response, the green sailors stayed exactly where they were, rooted to the spot and quaking in abject terror. Then they screamed and turned tail and ran for their little emerald lives. They were too well trained to openly disobey Smooth Cheeks by going below deck so they fell over themselves trying to find a hiding place.

Needless to say, they were a little bit scared.

Not so for the rest of Captain Speedster's crew. Yes, they were rubbish at building ships. Yes, they were even worse when it came to actually sailing ships – but when it came to defending the *Hogspignola* they didn't hesitate.

Squire Red was the first in the air. He flung himself overboard, flying towards the Octopig's hulking snout. The Hawkinses cheered – and then winced as he smacked into the monster's thick hide with a horrible crunching noise. He bounced off the beast, landing in a crumpled heap on the deck.

'What are we going to do?' asked Jay, but Jim had an idea.

'Use the sails,' he called down and grinned as Dr Matilda immediately caught his drift. The bird

threw herself into the main sail, which creaked as it took her weight. For a second Jim thought his plan wasn't going to work, but – TWANG! – Dr Matilda was catapulted towards the Octopig.

With a tremendous squawk, Dr Matilda produced the enormous frying pan she had been keeping tucked away in her feathers for emergencies and swung it around towards the creature.

TWAAANG!

The Octopig bellowed in surprise and let go of the ship. Dr Matilda tumbled back towards the deck. She landed in a cloud of feathers, but didn't stop to lick her wounds.

'No time to waste,' she yelled as she bounced back up for a second attempt. 'Throw everything we've got at it!'

That's exactly what the birds did. Dr Matilda and Squire Red repeatedly flung themselves at the Octopig's face, while Captain Speedster jumped on to the ship's wheel, spinning it round and round until he shot off like a bullet in the direction of the creature.

Meanwhile, another idea had occurred to Mr Bomb. 'Man the cannons!' he yelled, squeezing himself into the barrel of one of the large, bulky guns that lined the deck. Miss Stella and Mr Hal did the same while the Hawkinses leapt down from the crow's nest. As one, the three brothers lit the fuses and took a couple of steps back.

BOOM! BOOM! BOOM!

The guns shot the birds straight at the Octopig.

Stella slammed into one of the beast's tentacles, while Hal whipped around the back of the monster's massive head like a boomerang, slapping into the back of its huge skull.

Mr Bomb wasn't so lucky. With a horrible, wet splash he landed straight in the Octopig's right nostril. He wriggled and twisted but couldn't get free, getting angrier by the second.

The Hawkinses watched, amazed, as Bomb's black face turned red with rage and his entire body began to swell.

'Is there any reason he's called Mr Bomb?' Jay asked his brothers.

His question was answered as the steaming sailor burst into a blaze of light.

KER–BLAM!

The Octopig made the kind of noise that's only made by a giant sea monster who has just had an angry bird explode in its nasal passage. Bomb was blown clear and thrown on to the deck.

'You've maddened it,' yelped Smooth Cheeks,

as the Octopig lashed out, flipping the ship up as if it were a pancake. The *Hogspignola* shot up and then slowly started moving towards the creature's open mouth.

They were going to be swallowed whole!

The crew screamed, all except for Jay, who wrinkled his nose as a familiar smell wafted out of the open galley door. It was even more powerful than the stink of the Octopig.

'Quick,' he called to his brothers. 'Help me grab Smooth Cheeks's pot.'

'This is no time to think of food,' Jim pointed out.

'Especially Smooth Cheeks's slop,' added Jake.

'Trust me,' Jay said, bouncing through the door. The other two blue birds followed, desperately trying to avoid the pots and pans flying all over the place.

'We need to get this out on deck,' Jay instructed, grabbing the pot from the oven. Jim and Jake nipped underneath, taking the weight of the cauldron on their heads so that the vile mixture didn't slosh all over the floor.

Jim seized a handle. 'I still don't get why we're doing this.'

'You'll see,' said Jay, jumping down to join them. 'Smells like grass broth today.'

Jake pulled a face. 'Ugh! Gross!'

'Here's hoping. Come on!'

The three birds pushed the pot out of the galley on to the almost vertical deck, disgusting dollops of green gunge splashing over them.

'Let's give that eight-legged hog something to feast on,' Jay said, throwing the pot in the air.

The cauldron went straight down, pouring its vile contents into the monster's open mouth.

The beast gagged and gargled. It spat the broth back out, the spray of the regurgitated soup hitting the *Hogspignola* with such force that the ship hung for a moment, suspended in the air. Then the sails filled and, miraculously, they soared away from the retching Octopig. Far, far away.

The Hawkinses whooped and cheered, while Long John Smooth Cheeks hung on to the main mast for dear life.

'Waaaah!' he cried. 'Pigs aren't supposed to fly!'

'Which is OK,' hissed the sailor that looked suspiciously like Stinky, 'because you're a bird, remember?'

'Oh yes,' Smooth Cheeks said, glancing around to see if anyone had noticed, 'but I still don't likes it.'

'Land ahoy!' Dr Matilda called out, as the boat began to dip. Jim looked up. Sure enough the *Hogspignola* was dropping down, rushing straight towards a large egg-shaped island.

They were going to crash!

8

Easter Egg Island

'Abandon ship!' yelled Smooth Cheeks as the island rushed up to meet them. 'Chefs and pot-washers first!'

'No,' called out Jim. 'It's OK. We're going to overshoot. Look!'

Sure enough, the *Hogspignola* soared over the island, plunging into the water not far from the northern coast. The bow of the ship hit the surface, sending up a tremendous wave, but they were down and safe, if a little soggy.

'We made it,' chirped the Captain happily.

'N-never had any doubts,' groaned Smooth Cheeks, looking greener than ever.

'And did you see the island as we flew above it?' Dr Matilda asked, jumping up on to a nearby railing. 'It's egg-shaped!'

Jim, Jay and Jake leapt up beside her.

'Easter Egg Island,' they said together. 'We've found it.'

'It's smaller than I imagined,' Squire Red admitted. 'But look here –' he unrolled the map – 'we go ashore on this beach, make our way through these cliffs –' he pointed – 'and then through this valley until we get to those beaches . . .'

'The Scrambled Shores,' Smooth Cheeks interrupted.

'Yes,' Red said grumpily, 'everyone knows that. We set off at dawn. The early bird catches the long-lost treasure and all that.'

That night no one could eat, not just because of Smooth Cheeks's disgusting grub, but because they were all so excited.

Jim, Jay and Jake sat at the bow of the *Hogspinola*, gazing at the moon hanging low over the island.

'Just think,' Jim said. 'Captain Featherbeard's treasure is somewhere on that island, waiting to be discovered.'

'Our treasure, you mean,' Jay said. He glanced at Jake. 'Hey, what's wrong with you?'

Jake was peering towards the galley door. 'Can you hear snorting?'

Jim listened. Jake was right. There was grunting coming from the kitchens. 'Come on,' he said, 'maybe the others have finally found something to eat in those kitchens.'

The other two followed, sneaking into the smelly galley.

'Behind here,' Jim said, ducking behind a pile of crates.

The blue birds peered over the top of the wooden boxes, straining to see in the weak candlelight.

It was Long John Smooth Cheeks and the two

sailors who looked suspiciously like Pew and
Stinky. But they weren't eating.

'This is it, lads,' the sailor who looked like Stinky
said. 'First we deal with those bothersome birds ...'

'And then we grab the treasure,' said the
smaller one.

Smooth Cheeks's face lit up at the thought.
'Those lovely, juicy eggs. I can almost taste the
golden yolks. Oink!'

'Best of all,' said the sailor who looked
suspiciously like Pew, 'we'll be able to take off

these stupid disguises.' He flicked at his beak with his tongue, knocking it from his face to reveal a stubby, green snout. 'Ah, that's better.'

'They're not really birds,' Jim gasped in amazement. 'They're pigs!'

'I bet Smooth Cheeks isn't even a chef,' Jay whispered.

'To be honest, we should have guessed that bit as soon as we tasted his food,' Jake pointed out.

'We should have guessed it all,' said Jim. 'Let's tell Squire Red.'

'Yeah,' Jay agreed, 'informing the others would be the wise thing to do.'

'Or we could just attack them anyway,' pointed out Jake with a grin.

'GOOD PLAN!' the three shouted at once and leapt from their hiding place.

Sadly, the birds weren't quick enough. With a cry of 'Scatter!' the plotting pigs rolled out of the way and Jim, Jay and Jake found themselves flying into an open barrel.

They hit the bottom with a sharp smack and when they had untangled themselves, Smooth Cheeks was leering down at them.

'Well, looky here,' the treacherous hog sneered. 'What is we going to do with you three, eh?'

'We could cook 'em?' said the sailor who looked suspiciously like Pew because he actually was Pew.

Stinky pulled a face. 'Yuck! Roasted feathers. No thank you.'

'I've got meself a better idea,' said Long John Smooth Cheeks, fitting the lid on the barrel. 'Let's chuck 'em overboard. Oink!'

The birds were plunged into darkness. Worse, they could hear the sound of a hammer. In desperation, Jim threw himself at the lid, but it wouldn't budge.

'They must have nailed it shut,' he sighed, his head swimming.

'I think that's the least of our troubles,' Jay said as they felt the barrel being hoisted into the air.

The pigs were taking the barrel somewhere . . .

On deck, Smooth Cheeks giggled as Pew and Stinky rolled the keg to the side of the ship.

'Bye-bye birdies,' he grunted, giving it one final shove. The barrel tumbled over the edge and splashed into the murky waters far below.

'Right,' said Stinky. 'Now for the rest of the crew!'

Squire Red awoke with a start. Bleary-eyed,

he looked around the cabin. What was that sound? And, saying that, where were the rest of his bunkmates? He was alone in their cramped quarters.

Still half asleep, he tumbled from his hammock and bounced over to his cabin door – which, to be honest, didn't take him long considering the size of the room.

Yes, it sounded like a voice, but who would be singing at this time?

The deck outside was deserted, as was usual at night. Everyone should have been tucked up in bed, dreaming of going ashore in the morning.

Then who was singing so beautifully? And where were the Flock? In a daze, the Squire made his way across the moonlit deck, the haunting song filling his ears, driving him forward. It was so angelic. So bewitching. He had to find out who it was.

He hopped up the steps to the command deck and drew a sharp breath when he saw what was standing behind the steering wheel.

It was a mermaid. An honest-to-goodness, real-life mermaid with long golden hair and a shimmering tail stretched out beside her. She swayed as she sang, and Squire Red longed to see her properly. If she was half as beautiful as her voice . . .

'H–hello?' he said, his voice wavering more than he expected.

The mermaid started and fell silent.

'No,' he urged, leaping nearer. 'Don't stop singing. I didn't mean to scare you . . .'

'That's funny,' giggled the mermaid, spinning around, 'because I meant to scare you!'

Squire Red squawked in shock. The mermaid wasn't beautiful. Anything but. She wasn't even a she! An ugly green face leered out from beneath the dazzling hair and the iridescent tail was a fake.

'Long John Smooth Cheeks!' Red gasped, his eyes like saucers. 'But you're a . . . a . . .'

'Pig!' snorted Smooth Cheeks as a net dropped down over the Squire. 'And you be captured! Oink oink!'

Red struggled to free himself, but only ended up with the ropes tangling tighter than before.

'No!' he cried, as the rest of Smooth Cheeks's cronies appeared, no longer wearing their battered bird disguises. 'You can't all be pigs!'

'I'm afraid we is, my lord,' Smooth Cheeks chuckled, throwing off his wig. 'One hundred per cent prime pork.'

Pew and Stinky came shuffling from the shadows.

'You tricked 'im well and good, Captain,' said Stinky.

'C-captain?' stuttered the Squire. 'I thought you were a cook?'

'Ha!' Pew laughed. 'The Captain has never cooked a meal in 'is life. It was all lies.'

'But your references . . .' Red said. 'All those ships you served on . . .'

'You mean the Sea Snout, the Flying Sow and the Black Boar?' Smooth Cheeks reminded him.

'Yes!'

Smooth Cheeks bellowed with laughter. 'I didn't serve on 'em. I was their captain. Their pirate captain.'

'Pirates!' the Squire squeaked. 'Then all this time, you were just after . . .'

'The map,' said Pew, producing the scroll. 'I've gots it 'ere. Took it right from the Squire's quarters, sir. The eggs are as good as ours!'

'Ours?' snapped Smooth Cheeks.

'I means, as good as yours, Captain!' Pew said quickly.

Still tangled in the net, Red jutted out his beak defiantly. 'It doesn't matter. You may have captured me, but the rest of my Flock won't fall for the same sneaky trick.'

'Is that so?' Smooth Cheeks asked, glancing

at the rigging. Red followed his gaze to see Dr Matilda, Captain Speedster and the rest of the birds hanging sheepishly from similar nets.

'This is mutiny!' the Squire screamed, wriggling helplessly as he was hoisted up to join them.

'That it is, your lordship,' Smooth Cheeks crowed. 'Me piggy pirate plan has worked perfectly. Featherbeard's treasure shall be mine! All mine! Oink oink.'

9

Ben Hamm

Jim landed on top of his brothers with a thud.

'Ow!'

'Watch it,' snapped Jake.

'It's not going to work,' said Jay. 'You've been trying for hours.'

'I can't just give up,' said Jim, launching back up at the lid again. 'Who knows what Smooth Cheeks is up to? Help me, will you?'

The other two Hawkinses shrugged and joined in, flinging themselves at the underside of the lid. The barrel had stopped turning and tumbling a while back. They must have washed up on the island. The only problem was that the lid wouldn't budge.

The birds clattered around the inside of the cramped container, but it didn't make any difference.

'I give up,' Jay said.

'I wish I could see something,' said Jake. 'It's so dark in here.'

'Shhhhh,' Jim whispered. 'Someone's outside.'

Sure enough, they could hear the crump, crump, crump of someone bouncing across the sand towards them. Then they heard scratching and hammering directly overhead. Then silence. The Hawkinses hardly dared to breathe.

'Maybe they've gone,' Jake hissed.

'But who exactly is it?' Jay asked.

'We're about to find out!' said Jim.

Suddenly, there was a crack and the lid started to open and bright sunlight came streaming in, dazzling the birds. Then someone blocked the light. It was a green someone, with large staring eyes and a pronounced snout.

'PIG!' they yelled, jumping up at once. 'POP IT!'

They shot out of the barrel like rockets and slammed into the stranger, knocking him over.

'You're not having us for dinner, you cob-rolling creep,' shouted Jim, as they pounced on the petrified pig.

'Yeah, eat beak instead,' Jay added, pecking at the hog's ear.

Jake didn't say anything. He was too angry to even rant.

'Please stop,' pleaded the pig. 'I don't want to eat you. Why would I want to do such a thing?'

'Because you're a stinking swashbuckling swine,' Jay yelled, starting on the other ear. 'One of the dastardly double-crossers who threw us off the ship.'

'No, I'm not,' the pig squealed. 'Please don't hurt me.'

So, the Hawkinses stopped, if only to get their breath back. They stood glaring at the bruised boar picking itself up from the sand. He had a huge dome-like forehead complete with unruly white eyebrows and the deepest worry lines the birds had ever seen. A pair of cracked spectacles dangled from his snout and he wore a red flower tucked behind his ears. It had lost most of its petals. The tools he'd used to free the birds lay scattered around them. The Hawkinses didn't recognize this pig from the *Hogspignola*, but pigs do all look the same.

'Thank you,' the stranger said, straightening

his glasses. 'I mean you no harm. My name is Ben Hamm.'

'Of course you mean us harm,' said Jake, finally calming down enough to talk. 'You're a pig. Pigs hate birds. Birds hate pigs. Those are the rules.'

'Not for me,' Ben said, licking one of his lenses clean with his tongue. 'Yes, I used to be a pirate ...'

'I knew it,' shouted Jay, ready for another round of boar battering.

'But I gave all that up,' Ben added quickly. 'I only became a pirate in the first place because my old dad was a pirate before me, and his dad was a pirate before him, and his dad's dad was a pirate before his dad and –'

'OK, we get the idea,' cut in Jake.

'It just wasn't for me,' said Ben. 'All that plundering and pillaging. Never had my heart in it, to be honest. I'd rather potter around in my garden.'

'OK,' said Jim doubtfully. 'I suppose you don't sound much like a pirate.'

'I was the worst pirate in the entire history of piracy,' Ben Hamm said, looking quite pleased with himself. 'At least that's what my old captain, Long John Smooth Cheeks, used to say . . .'

'Smooth Cheeks was your captain?' Jay gasped.

A shadow passed over Ben's piggy face. 'I'm afraid so. He marooned me here years ago, when I refused to go on a raid because I wanted to water my petunias. Said I was a disgrace to the snout and crossbones. All he cared about was finding Captain Featherbeard's lost treasure . . .'

'And you didn't help him?' Jake asked.

'Of course not,' Ben Hamm said. 'Featherbeard's eggs are the rarest in the world. They're beautiful, like no other eggs known to piggykind. If they were discovered, they'd be nothing but trouble. Piggy pirate crews would be at each others' snouts to get to them.'

'All Smooth Cheeks wants to do is scoff them,' said Jim.

Ben sighed. 'It's such a waste. I think the eggs

should be left where they are, safe and sound.'

'But Smooth Cheeks is on his way!' said Jim, explaining about Billy Beak's map and the Hogspignola and the pigs in disguise.

'I know,' Ben said grimly, as Jim finished the story. 'I'm afraid Smooth Cheeks's revolting raiders are already ashore.'

'Where?' growled Jim, his beak set in a hard line.

'I'll show you,' said Ben, hopping down the beach. 'This way!'

'There they are,' Ben whispered, peering over a large sand dune. 'I hoped never to see that lot again.'

The Hawkinses jostled behind him, their beaks dropping at the sight.

The *Hogspignola* was moored just off the beach and the pigs had made camp further up on high ground. A dinghy ferrying a large, blimp-like figure so heavy that he threatened to sink the small boat was being rowed ashore by a couple of pirates.

'Smooth Cheeks,' growled Jake, his eyes boring into the tubby traitor. The chef's headgear was gone, replaced by a velvet hat with a glittering snout and crossbones emblazoned on the front, a ridiculously large feather tucked jauntily into the brim.

A group of puny pirates raced up to their leader and hauled him on to their shoulders, carrying him towards a big wooden cage in the middle of the camp.

The Hawkinses beaks curled into snarls when their furious eyes fell upon the cage. Inside were Red, Dr Matilda, Captain Speedster and the rest of the crew. Trapped, and at Smooth Cheeks's mercy. The birds were crammed in tighter than one of Billy Beak's tins of sardines, completely unable to move. They needed rescuing and they needed rescuing now!

'It's bacon-bashing time,' said Jake, ready to throw himself into the fray.

'No,' said Ben urgently. 'Don't get in such a flap. You really shouldn't just rush ahead without thinking.'

'But that's what we always do,' insisted Jim.

'Yes, and how did you like the barrel?' the former pirate asked.

The birds shuffled in silence, not able to think of an answer.

'Trust me,' said Ben. 'There's a better way.'

'Better than pounding a pack of pig pirates?' Jay said, not believing a word of it. 'You're still on their side, aren't you?'

Ben shook his head. 'I promise you I'm not. I'd like to see Smooth Cheeks taught a lesson as much as anyone – but you're not going to help your friends by getting yourselves captured.'

'So what should we do?' asked Jim.

A grin spread across Ben's wrinkled face. A particularly devious grin. 'Prick up your ears, my little feathered friends. I have a plan.'

The Hawkinses moved closer.

'How do you feel about dressing up?' he asked.

10

The Plan

Night had fallen on the pigs' camp, not that the birds had managed to get much sleep in their cage. The pirates had worked late into the evening, building a very large and very complicated digging machine. There had been banging and sawing and grunting and squealing until the wee small hours.

Stinky seemed very pleased with himself. Apparently his official steam-powered, reinforced piggy dig-a-tron was his best work yet.

'We need to get out of here,' complained Captain Speedster, shoving Dr Matilda's crest off his face.

'Of course we do,' snapped the Squire. 'But how?'

'I could try exploding again,' suggested Mr Bomb.

'NO!' everyone answered. The big black bird had tried that trick a couple of hours ago. The cage had remained intact although the birds had lost quite a few feathers in the blast.

Miss Stella noticed something – or rather someone – creeping across the camp. 'What about these three runts?' she suggested. 'Perhaps we could trick them into releasing us.'

The Squire struggled to turn around, accidentally poking Dr Matilda in the eye with his beak. Three small piglets were heading in their direction.

'Have you ever seen such piddling pigs?' said the Squire.

'No,' Dr Matilda replied, her eye still throbbing. 'Their snouts look rubbish too, like they're made out of cardboard or something.'

'They're not even very green,' added Captain Speedster. 'In fact, in this moonlight, they look a bit blue.'

'I know what to do,' said Mr Hal, coughing loudly. 'Hey, you three,' he called, in a gruff voice that was obviously supposed to sound like a pig. 'It's me, Long John Smooth Cheeks. Those idiots Pew and Stinky locked me up with the birds! Let me out.'

'Nice try, Mr Hal,' said the first small blue pig, hopping on to the head of one of the others, 'but you're not fooling anyone.'

'Then what are you doing?' asked the Squire, as the third piglet leapt on top of the other two to reach the lock.

'Letting you out of the cage, of course,' he whispered, shoving a oddly shaped key into the lock.

'Why would you do that?' asked Dr Matilda.

'Because it's us,' said the middle piglet, shoving aside his fake snout. 'Jim, Jay and Jake.'

The birds cheered. In fact, Mr Bomb got so excited he exploded again. By the time everyone stopped choking on the smoke, the lock had been sprung.

'Ben's skeleton key worked!' said Jim, hopping down from Jay's head.

'Who?' asked the slightly scorched Squire.

'Our friend,' answered Jay, hopping down from Jake's head.

'He's the one hiding over there,' said Jake.

'Where?' asked Speedster.

'At the edge of the camp,' said Jim.

The birds all looked where Jim was pointing.

'You mean the sorry-looking soul surrounded by snarling pirates?' asked Dr Matilda.

The Hawkinses spun around. Sure enough, Ben had been discovered by Smooth Cheeks's crew and was staring nervously at the razor-sharp cutlasses pointing in his general direction.

'Any chance of a rescue, lads?' he asked, sweat pouring down his brow.

He didn't have to ask twice. The entire Flock leapt forward as one, with the Hawkinses in the lead.

'We'll save you, Ben!' the chicks said at once. 'GET THOSE GRUNTERS!'

The battle was intense. Freed from their cage, the birds sprung into action, beaks flashing and heads butting. The pigs didn't stand a chance. They may have been devious but in a straight fight the pathetic porkers were no match for the furious

feathered Flock. Dr Matilda's frying pan clanged
this way and that, Mr Bomb blew his top over
and over again, and Captain Speedster charged
headfirst, popping any pirates in his path.

Even the sword-wielding swine around Ben
Hamm didn't stand much chance. Squire Red

lowered his head and charged forward, sending each pig flying like pirate-shaped skittles (which admittedly isn't a practical shape for a skittle in the first place).

'Thankee,' said Ben. 'But you need to do something about that contraption.' He pointed at the official steam-powered, reinforced piggy dig-a-tron. It loomed above them, a jumbled tower of hissing hydraulics and wonky winches. Some bits were constructed from wood, others from rock, all tottering on a set of wheels that allowed it to be pushed from location to location.

As they watched, steam shot out of pipes and gears ground against each other, ready to power half a dozen spades that jutted down to the ground like weird shovel-like teeth.

'It's crude, I admit,' said Ben, 'but with it they'll be able to find the eggs. Pigs are very good at finding eggs.'

'Not if we have anything to do with it,' Red snapped. 'Mr Hal, Miss Stella – do your thing!'

So they did. Mr Hal swung around from behind to smash the chimney, while Miss Stella surprised everyone by blowing bubbles that lifted the machine's foundations clear of the rocky plateau it was built on.

'There she blows,' cheered Captain Speedster.

With an almighty crash the official steam-powered, reinforced piggy dig-a-tron toppled over, straight on to the remaining buccaneering boars.

'Ha ha,' laughed Ben, pulling off a rather peculiar piggy dance of victory. 'That'll learn 'em. Piracy never pays. Except when you discover piles and piles of gold and treasure, of course,' he added sheepishly.

'Treasure!' echoed the Squire. 'The map? Where's the map?'

'Smooth Cheeks had it,' said Speedster, dashing around to find the podgy pirate in the dig-a-tron wreckage. 'But where is the fat pig?'

The traitorous pirate captain was nowhere to be seen.

'Oink. You'll never find 'im,' giggled Pew from beneath a broken beam. 'He sneaked off as soon as you attacked.'

'Yeah,' sniffed Stinky, who was still upset about his contraption's collapse, 'and he's taken those horrible chicks with him!'

'What?' Ben said, his eyes spreading wide with panic. 'He's taken the Hawkins?'

The birds looked everywhere, but the pigs were right – Smooth Cheeks and the blue birds had vanished.

11

X Marks the Spot

On the south-eastern side of the island, Long John Smooth Cheeks was sweating. In addition to his heavy backpack, he was dragging the Hawkinses along behind him.

Tied together with a heavy rope, the birds bounced off rocks and stones as Smooth Cheeks followed Featherbeard's map through a narrow valley.

'We be nearly there,' the treacherous swine grunted, his piggy eyes brimming with excitement. 'Just around this corner.'

After they'd been dragged over a particularly rough patch of shingle, Jim cried, 'Why do you need us? You've got the map!'

'What?' Smooth Cheeks said, glancing back at

them. 'You expect me to digs the treasure up by meself? Besides I wants to see your little birdy faces when I gobbles all the eggs. Oink oink!'

'Noooooooooooo!' wailed a voice from above.

'W-what be that?' Smooth Cheeks said, stopping so abruptly that the Hawkinses bumped straight into his curly tail.

'Turn baaaaaaaaack!' howled something else, this time from behind.

The pig and the birds huddled close to each other, teeth and beaks chattering in fear.

'P-perhaps the legends were true,' Jim said, gulping. 'Perhaps the island is haunted.'

'B-but you said there's no such thing as ghosts,' Jay reminded him.

'He's been wrong before,' pointed out Jake.

'Have not.'

'Have too.'

'Have not.'

'Have tooooooo,' mimicked a ghostly white pig popping up from behind a rock.

Smooth Cheeks squealed in fright as more spectres appeared all around.

'Aaaaaaah!' Smooth Cheeks screamed and began running around hysterically. 'We're doomed! Doomed, I tells ye. Someone save old Smooth Cheeks's bacon, please!'

The Hawkinses couldn't answer. They were too busy being spun around on the end of the rope. The more the pig panicked, the more the birds twirled, round and round and round.

'Look out,' Jay screamed. 'You're going to send us smashing into the spooks that Jim said didn't exist.'

'Too late,' Jake called out, as they ploughed into the first phantom. 'Ow! That hurt!'

'So did that,' said Jim as they smashed into the next. And the next and the next.

'These haunts are rock-hard,' gasped Jay, as they shattered another spirit.

'I'm not surprised,' said Jake. 'They're made of stone!'

'Stone?' Smooth Cheeks repeated, stopping

in his tracks and looking around. Sure enough, each and every ghost was made of granite, painted white and hung from dropping springs.

'But what about the spooky voices?'

Smooth Cheeks nudged a fake bush aside with his snout. 'This might have something to do with it.' The swine had revealed an old gramophone player linked to a complex series of pulleys and ropes.

'So when the so-called spectres shot up . . .' Jay said.

'They turned on the voices on the record player,' said Jim. 'It was all a trick.'

'Featherbeard must have left them behind,' said Jake. 'To scare away egg-hunters.'

'Told you they weren't real,' sniffed Jim.

'But why ghosts?' asked Smooth Cheeks. 'Pigs aren't superstitious.'

'Yeah, but they are incredibly stupid,' sniggered Jay to Jim.

If Smooth Cheeks heard the jibe, he didn't react.

'Trick or not, they mean we're nearly there,'

cried out the pirate, racing along the path. 'What are we waiting for? Oink oink.'

'Here we go again,' said Jake, as they were dragged after him towards the beach.

After what seemed like hours, Smooth Cheeks stopped.

'This must be it!' he cried. They were at the southernmost tip of the island, and were surrounded by seemingly endless golden sands – and the occasional crab.

'How can you tell?' asked Jake.

'Because X marks the spot, lad,' declared Smooth Cheeks, shoving the map beneath their beaks. A big, black X was written on the parchment and, when the pirate pulled the map aside, the Hawkinses could see a similar, even bigger X painted on the sand itself.

'Not as subtle as I'd imagined,' said Jay, raising an eyebrow.

'Who cares!' replied Smooth Cheeks, giving out the spades he'd been carrying in the backpack. 'Get digging!'

The Hawkinses went to work, sweating under the heat of the morning sun.

'Don't worry,' whispered Jim, as they toiled. 'I have a plan.'

'Does it involve smashing old Smooth Cheeks into a pulp with our shovels?' asked Jay hopefully.

'No,' said Jim. 'Remember what Ben taught us. Don't get in a flap. We'll dig down, find the treasure chest and then we'll decide what to do.'

'Brilliant,' said Jake. 'Let's hope the treasure isn't buried too deep.'

It was a vain hope. The birds kept digging and digging. And then they dug a little bit more for good measure.

Finally, Jay's spade struck something hard.

'It's the treasure!' he called out and the three of them started scrabbling with their beaks. Before long they could make out the shape of a lid –

and then an entire casket. Jay had been right. 'Featherbeard's chest! The secret stash of top-secret eggs must be inside!'

There was a shout of 'Incoming!' and Long John Smooth Cheeks plummeted down towards them. They tried to scrabble out of the way but the walls of the hole were too steep.

With a loud, heavy thwack! the podgy pirate landed right on top of them.

'This be it!' he yelled, already salivating at the thought of the feast hidden inside the chest.

'Featherbeard's treasure, after all these years – and it's mine. All mine. Oink, oink, oink!'

'Are you sure about that?' called a familiar voice.

'Eh?' said Smooth Cheeks glancing up, straight into the angry eyes of Squire Red.

'Ha!' he jeered. 'What are you going to do about it, birdbrain? You be up there, and I be down here. You've lost.'

'You're right,' Red said, peering over the edge.

'I am up here, and so are my friends.'

Smooth Cheeks swallowed as more faces appeared at the top of the pit. Dr Matilda. Captain Speedster. Mr Bomb, and all the rest. They glared at him, one thought on all their minds.

'Now, let's not be hasty, m'lord,' whimpered Smooth Cheeks, his bottom lip wobbling. 'We could always parlay. One or two eggs for ye, a dozen or so for me. Sounds fair, don't it?'

'Hmmmm, let me think about that,' said the Squire.

Smooth Cheeks's face brightened hopefully.

'OK,' Red announced with a grin, 'thought about it.'

'We has a deal?' asked Smooth Cheeks.

'Nope! GET HIM!'

As one, the Flock jumped into the hole and fell upon Smooth Cheeks in a blur of frenzied feathers.

12

The Treasure

Thirty seconds later and Smooth Cheeks was tied up in the very same rope he'd used on the Hawkinses.

'But where are the boys?' asked Dr Matilda. 'What has Smooth Cheeks done with them?'

'Mfffl–mffr!' The sound seemed to be coming from underneath Long John Smooth Cheeks's restrained body. Hal flipped the swine over to reveal three black and blue chicks gasping for breath.

'That was horrible,' wheezed Jake.

'I never want to be squashed beneath a swine again,' groaned Jay.

'Don't worry about that,' Jim said. 'What about the treasure?'

The Flock turned to face the chest, Red frowning when he took in the large lock. 'How do we get it open?'

'I could blow it open?' suggested Bomb.

'NO!' yelled everyone else.

'What about Ben's skeleton key?' asked Jay. Jake grinned, pulling it out from behind his back, before his face crumpled in disappointment.

'It's broken,' he said, brandishing the snapped key. 'Must have happened in the fight.'

'Then all is lost,' wailed Dr Matilda.

'Of course it isn't,' a voice called down from above. 'The wretched thing's already open.'

They all looked up to see Ben Hamm grinning down at them. 'Go on,' he said. 'Flip the lid. Take a look.'

Squire Red turned to the Hawkinses. 'I think the honour should be yours,' he said, stepping aside.

Sharing nervous glances, the three chicks hopped forward, slipped their beaks beneath the lid and threw it open.

Every bird in the hole gasped as Ben broke into peals of piggy laughter.

The treasure chest was empty!

'What?' said Jim.

'How?' said Jake.

'Again?' said Jay.

'You!' roared the Squire glaring up at Ben Hamm. 'You knew the eggs were gone! You've taken them.'

The pig nodded happily. 'Yes. Yes, I have.'

Red's feathers stood on end and his eyes flashed the same colour as his plumage. The other birds shuffled back, making space for the outburst that was sure to come. The Squire looked like the angriest bird in a long line of angry birds and poor old Ben Hamm was to bear the brunt of his outrage. Red pulled back, ready to spring from the hole and . . . the Hawkinses leapt forward to stop him.

'Wait!' said Jake. 'You need to calm down!'

'Yeah,' agreed Jay. 'Sometimes you need to think before flying off the handle.'

Jim turned and looked up at his friend.

'Ben, why did you take the eggs out of the chest?'

Ben beamed down at the wise little chick.

'Come with me . . .' he said.

'Wahoo!' the Hawkinses cheered, as Ben led them into a nearby cave piled high with eggs

of all different shapes and sizes. Well, the objects were smooth, gleaming and shaped like eggs. But they were perfectly golden and they seemed to shimmer.

'I discovered Featherbeard's secret stash long, long ago,' Ben explained, 'when I first came to the island. I knew that it would be trouble . . .'

'So you brought the eggs here,' said Dr Matilda, gazing up at the shining heap.

'There was always a chance they'd be found buried beneath the sand,' Ben nodded. 'This way I thought they'd be safe.'

'But the pigs have found out they're on the island,' Jim chipped in. 'They'll just get reinforcements and come back.'

'Yes, Smooth Cheeks and his pirate piggies may be battered for now, but they'll soon be up to their old tricks,' Ben said, hopping over to the Squire, who was nuzzling against one of the precious shells. 'Will you take them?'

'Us?' said Red.

'You've seen how beautiful they are,' Ben said. 'I couldn't bear to think of them poached, scrambled, fried or boiled.'

Squire Red nodded, his feathers puffing up as he made a decision. 'We'll take them as far away from here as we can sail,' he said, 'and bury them where no one will find them again.'

Their minds made up, the birds hurried back to the empty chest to haul it out of the hole. It took longer than they expected because Captain Speedster dropped it on the still dazed Long John Smooth Cheeks by accident.

They dragged it back to the cave, crammed all the eggs back into the chest and headed back to the Hogspignola. As they boarded the ship they waved happily at the pirate pigs, who were still struggling to get out from beneath the wreckage of the official steam-powered, reinforced piggy dig-a-tron.

'Enjoy your new home,' Ben shouted cheerfully as the anchor was raised and the

Hawkinses steered the boat away.

'So where are we going to hide the stash?' asked Squire Red, perched on top of Captain Featherbeard's chest. 'Another island?'

'Too obvious, isn't it?' said Dr Matilda.

A thought occurred to Jim. 'What about Billy Beak's cave? He promised to keep the eggs safe in the first place.'

'An egg-cellent plan,' said Captain Speedster, who had been waiting for the entire story to crack that atrocious pun.

'So that is what they did,' said Matilda, bringing her tale to a close. 'They sailed off into the horizon, Captain Featherbeard's treasure safe forever from the clutches of pesky pirates and pilfering pigs.'

'Wow!' sighed Jim with a smile.

'But what happened to Long John Smooth Cheeks and the rest of the pirate pigs?' asked Jay.

'They were marooned on the island,' said

Matilda gravely, 'with only sand to eat. Which is how the sandwich was invented, but that's another story . . .'

'You made that last bit up,' sniggered Jake.

'Maybe I did,' said Matilda, 'maybe I didn't, but the important thing is, have you learned anything from the story?'

Much to Matilda's delight, the Blues nodded enthusiastically.

'Oh yes,' they said as one. 'A big lesson.'

Matilda clucked with joy. 'That it never pays to rush off without thinking? That you should look before you leap?'

'Nah!' shouted Jay, suddenly running forward so fast that he knocked the white bird flying. 'All we've learned is that there's treasure out there somewhere . . .'

'Piles and piles of precious eggs that need protecting,' said Jay, trampling Matilda as he tore after his brother.

'And we're going to find them!' added Jim, kicking up dust as he raced out of the nest. 'Thanks, Matilda!'

Matilda watched them go and let out a long, weary sigh. Some things never change.

Then again, finding hidden treasure did sound very exciting . . .

'Hang on, boys,' Matilda called, chasing after the Blues. 'Wait for me . . .'

Who's Who?

Jim, Jake and Jay Hawkins – The three brothers are always on the lookout for a great adventure. After hearing the swashbuckling tales of Billy Beak, they long for their own escapades. They set sail with the suspicious-looking crew of the *Hogspignola* on a dangerous mission to find the long-buried treasure of the legendary Captain Featherbeard.

Billy Beak – Retired from sailing the Seven Seas, this old bird lives alone in a damp cave. Some think he is rather rude and grumpy, but the Hawkinses can't get enough of his stories. But be careful not to cross him . . . or you might feel the sharp end of his beak!

Squire Red – A rich dignitary who funds the trip to Easter Egg Island and leads the expedition. Squire Red is fearless and can always be found in the front line of any battle.

Captain Speedster – A bright yellow bird, who does everything at high speed. Unfortunately, he loses concentration very easily, so he doesn't always get it right.

Dr Matilda – A local doctor who joins the expedition to Easter Egg Island. She can always be relied upon to provide practical information.

Long John Smooth Cheeks – Long John Smooth Cheeks disguises himself as a humble ship's cook whose specialty is grass! Speedster's crew believe he is a bird but it's not long before the Hawkinses discover he is actually a piggy pirate!

Stinky – A shipmate and sidekick of Long John Smooth Cheeks, this pig cannot be trusted. Known for his shoddily-built contraptions, if there is a whiff of trouble in the air Stinky can usually be found at the centre of it.

Who's Who?

Pew – Wherever you find Stinky, you can be sure that Pew won't be far behind. Distinguished by his brightly coloured bandana, this cowardly pig follows Smooth Cheeks's orders to the letter.

Ben Hamm – A marooned castaway, Ben was once a pirate on Long John Smooth Cheeks's ship. But unlike the others, this pig doesn't enjoy being a pirate. He likes nothing more than tending to his petunias.

The Octopig – A creature of legend with eight tentacles and colossal eyes, it smells very, very rotten. The Octopig was once defeated by Billy Beak, but raises his ugly head once again . . .

Treasure Island
The Quiz

1. Who wrote the original *Treasure Island*?

(a) Lewis Carroll

(b) Robert Louis Stevenson

(c) Roald Dahl

2. What's the name of the ship they board to go to Easter Egg Island?

(a) The *Hogspignola*

(b) HMS *Pigtory*

(c) The *Titanic*

3. What is Billy Beak's favourite food?

(a) Eggs

(b) Tinned sardines

(c) Toast

4. What eight-tentacled creature attacks the ship?

(a) The Octopig

(b) The Octodog

(c) The Octobird

5. What is the name of the marooned pirate on Easter Egg Island?

(a) Ben Spam

(b) Ben Jam

(c) Ben Hamm

6. Who buried the top-secret eggs?

a) Captain Featherbeard

b) Captain Pigstache

c) Captain Hogfuzz

7. What does Ben Hamm prefer to being a pirate?

a) Swimming

b) Gardening

c) Flying

8. What's the name of the lost city discovered by Billy Beak?

a) Shell Dorado

b) Piglantis

c) Machu Pigchu

Pirate Facts

- As long as there have been ships . . . there have been pirates! Piracy was a big problem for ancient civilizations such as the Egyptians, Greeks and Romans.
- The best time and place in history to be a pirate was probably in the Caribbean from about 1560 to 1730.
- Pirates of this era really did wear earrings and bandanas, and had wooden legs or hooks as hands because many of them lost limbs in battle.
- Pirates didn't get paid; instead they shared out the treasure between themselves.
- Not all pirates were men. There have been many famous female pirates, such as Mary Read and Anne Bonny in the early 1700s.
- The 'Jolly Roger' flag, with white skull and crossbones, was a way to frighten other ships.
- 19 September is International Talk like a Pirate Day. Oooh-arrr, me hearties!

Pirate Pursuits

- Draw your own treasure map of Easter Egg Island. Remember X marks the spot!
- Imagine that Ben Hamm kept a diary during his time marooned on Easter Egg Island. Write some of the entries he may have made.
- Make up pirate names for yourself and your friends! Simply take your first name (or your middle name, or even another name entirely) and pick one of the words below to add to it.

Bloodstain ⭑ *Bloodthirsty* ⭑ *Bloody* ⭑ *Blackbeard* ⭑ *Bones* ⭑ *Cannonball* ⭑ *Castaway* ⭑ *Pegleg* ⭑ *Silver* ⭑ *Swashbuckling* ⭑

For example, you might become Holly Pegleg!

Cheep Laughs!

Q. Why does it take pirates so long to learn the alphabet?
A. *Because they spend years at C.*

Q. Why couldn't the pirate play cards?
A. *Because he was standing on the deck!*

Q. When is the best time for a pirate to buy a new ship?
A. *When it's on sail.*

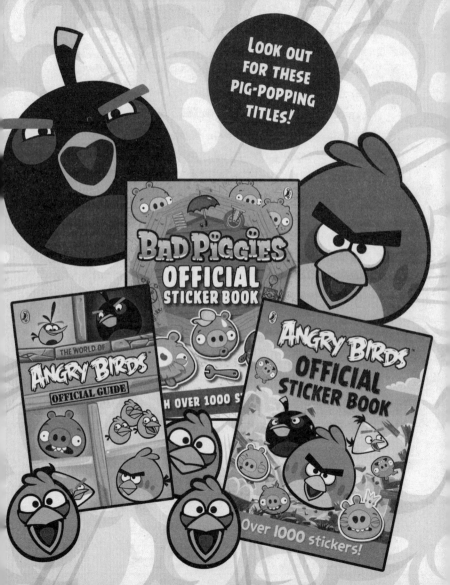

AN A–Z OF ADVENTURE...

Alice, Black Beauty, Cathy, Dracula, Estella, Fagin, Gulliver,
Huckleberry Finn, It, Jim Hawkins, King Arthur, Long John Silver, Mowgli,
Nancy, Oliver, Pollyanna, the Queen of Hearts, Ratty, Sara Crewe,
Tom Sawyer, Uriah Heep, Rip Van Winkle, the Wizard of Oz,
the PhoeniX, the Yahoos and Zeus...

Some of these you might know. Others you won't. Some you'll know without even knowing how you know them. They're from a cast of classic characters who have travelled through time – in their ships or motor cars, or even tumbled down rabbit holes – to come to life for your grandparents, your parents and now for you. These characters are so vivid and so exciting that they literally jump off the page and into your life. And it's completely up to you what they look like.

They're Puffin Classics for a reason.
It's because they're the best.

Puffin has been publishing the most innovative and imaginative children's literature for generations. From Mowgli to Merlin, Peter Pan to Pollyanna, no matter what your age or what you're into, wherever you see that little bird you'll be introduced to a whole host of new faces and amazing places.

PUFFIN CLASSICS